ST. MARY'S PUBLIC LIBRARY
127 Center Street
St. Marys, PA 15857
814 834-6141
email: library@stmaryslibrary.org
www.stmaryslibrary.org

Wishing you all the very best! Thanks for all your support. ♡

Di

KIBBLE
The Monarch Caterpillar Afraid to Get Wings

by Anita Gnan

Illustrations by John Fraser

I just love the moment right before the sun rises. It's quiet, and yet there's a brand new day starting. You can do a lot with a brand new day. Hear that? The first bird of the day—sounds like Larry. Yeah, that's definitely Larry. Larry's usually the first bird of the day. Come to think of it, he's usually the last bird of the day, too—I seriously have no idea when that guy sleeps. He's a great friend with lots of interesting stories to share and you can read along if you'd like. Just listen for this sound right here. When you hear it, turn the page, and you'll be all set. I'll see you a little later in the story. Enjoy.

I flew over a place the other day that stirred feelings I had never felt before. Since I didn't have much to do that day, I decided to make circles in the sky.

At first, I flew high above the trees, then down low over the water. The morning sun felt warm on my black wings and there were all sorts of beautiful wildflowers. Their colors popped blue, white, yellow, and red—but in all those wildflowers, there was one catching my eye that day—the milkweed.

I only bring it up because it has to do with this story I'm about to share with you. See, it was because of my interest in that patch of milkweed that I noticed something.

It was just a speck under one of those milkweed plants, but for some reason, this didn't seem quite right to me. So, I dove down and sat upon a nearby branch to have a closer look.

First Edition

Author: Anita Gnan | Illustrator: John Fraser | Editor: Victoria L. Stanish | Audio: Roy Gnan and Anita Gnan
Audiobook Voice Talent: Larry: Eric Geller | Kibble: Ciscandra Nostalghia | Samantha: Anita Gnan | Red: Roy Gnan
and featuring the whistling of Geert Chatrou

www.WestCreekMedia.com

ISBN: 978-0-9964735-0-7
LCCN: 2015909162

Printed in the United States of America

WCM

Only then did I notice it wasn't a speck at all, but a tiny little Monarch caterpillar. He couldn't have been more than a few days old. I must have scared him, too, because do you know what he said to me in the smallest of voices I have ever heard? He said...

"Please don't eat me."

Well, I thought that was funny, because I'm a blackbird, and every blackbird knows not to eat a Monarch caterpillar. So, of course, I told him the reason why.

"I'm not going to eat you, Kid. You're poisonous to me."

"I am?"

"You sure are."

Now that the little feller knew he'd make me very sick if I ate him, he was no longer afraid of me, so I decided to introduce myself.

"Larry's the name, and you are?"

"Kibble."

"Nice to meet you, Kibble. Say, why are you way down there on the ground? Shouldn't you be nibbling on all that tasty milkweed above you?"

"Oh, that's all right, I'm not very hungry."

"Wait a minute—a caterpillar who doesn't want to eat? Why, I never heard of such a thing. How do you expect to shed, my friend, if you don't eat?"

"Shed?"

"Yes, indeed. You'll end up eating so much milkweed that you'll shed your skin anywhere from four to six times."

"You mean I won't have any skin!"

"Oh—no, you'll have skin, little buddy. Shedding is a good thing. Each time you do, you're getting ready to build your chrysalis."

"My chrys-a-what?"

"Your chrysalis—your digs, my friend. A comfy little home where you can relax and let the fun of metamorphosis begin."

"Met-a-mor-fo-what?"

"Metamorphosis. Caterpillars all go through it. It's what makes them butterflies and moths you see today. In my opinion, though, the cool part about metamorphosis is that when it's over, you'll have your very own set of wings. They'll look a lot different than mine, of course, but the point is, you'll be able to fly."

I suppose, at this point, I was expecting Kibble to smile. I mean, I just told him he was going to be able to fly. But you know something? He didn't look the least bit excited.

I thought maybe he didn't hear me, so I stretched my wings out as far as they would go. I flapped them and flipped them, you know, just to show him how great wings are. I waited for him to smile, but he just sat there, all wide-eyed and staring at me.

Now, what happens next is something I'd rather not tell you about, but since it's part of the story, I'm going to leave it in. See, I was so set on getting Kibble to smile that I—well—I started making funny poses with my wings. I know, I know, not my finest hour. I tried hanging ten like a "Surfer Dude," then I flexed my muscles to look like "Hercules," but my saddest attempt to get a smile was my "Egyptian Pharaoh" pose. I don't even want to show you that one.

Thankfully, I don't think Kibble saw it either, because somewhere in the middle of all that posing, he had turned from me to look up at the sky. Kibble sat there staring at the sky for quite a while, too. I almost asked him if he was feeling all right, but then, Kibble asked me a very strange question.

"Is there a way to not get wings?"

"Not that I know of. Why do you ask, my friend?"

"Oh, no reason. Just—it looks so big up there."

I didn't know what to say to the little feller. His eyes were wide and his face looked—well, it looked to me like there might be a lot more going on with this little caterpillar than he was letting on.

Now at the time, I didn't know much about Monarch caterpillars, but I did know this—Kibble needed to eat to have enough strength to build his chrysalis and survive metamorphosis.

So, to give myself some time to think, I jumped on a milkweed plant and bent it down to Kibble. It's a good thing I did, too, because he was hungry. Kibble tore into eating a bunch of leaves, and while he did, I thought about what he had said about the size of the sky. I also thought about what I would want to hear if I was Kibble.

After all that thinking, what I decided was, when it comes right down to it, I always like to hear the truth. So I looked up at the sky and tried to see it like Kibble was seeing it.

> "You know something, Kibble, you're right—the sky sure does look big. That's probably because it is big, but the funny thing is, the same can be said about the ground when you're up there looking down here."

I laughed and laughed because there was so much truth in it, and I wanted more than anything to show him. I even offered to fly him up. You know, to give him a sneak peek of what's to come.

"Oh—uh—no thank you."

"Just a thought, just a thought. It is a beautiful day, after all, and there's nothing quite like hanging on a thermal on a sunny day like today—no, nothing quite like it."

"What's a thermal?"

"What's a thermal? Why, it's when the wind gets going just right and you power into full speed, and then you—release."

"You mean you poo?"

"No, Kid! What do I look like, a pigeon? I'm talking no flapping of your wings necessary. The wind becomes your sail."

"Oh—of course. It sounds really—fun."

There was something about the way Kibble said that last word. It sort of sounded like he didn't think it would be fun at all.

Around that time, my friend Samantha came along. Sam and I go way back. She's real smart. She even taught me how to catch worms. Now that's an odd thing for Sam to know about because she's a rat, but I'll save that story for another day.

"Talking altitude again, Larry?"

"You know it, my friend, you know it. Hey, Sam, this is Kibble. He's going up someday."

"Let me guess, in three to four weeks, right? Hi, Kid. Are you guys coming by the yard today?"

"No, no, not today. I was just telling Kibble here about thermals."

"Ah yes, thermals. I'm afraid it's lost on me, Kid. I'll take a good sewer that's dark and wet from day-old rainwater any day over a thermal. Sometimes I even find food there. Today is the perfect example. Take a look at this special sewer surprise I found last night."

I forgot to warn Kibble about looking too closely at one of Sam's special sewer surprises. I only remembered myself as she was opening her peanut-shaped lunchbox. Well, I quickly threw my head back to avoid the horrible-smelling, bluish-green blob oozing there in front of us, but poor Kibble got a real good whiff.

He started gagging and I thought for sure he was going to throw up the milkweed he had eaten earlier, but somehow Kibble managed to keep it down. Funny thing is, Sam didn't even notice our reaction to her sewer surprise. She just stood there in awe of it. Then she said...

"I'm not entirely sure what it is, of course, but that's what makes it a surprise. I think I'll scrape off the fuzzy white coating and save that for later. I can give you some if you'd like."

"Yeah—thanks, Sam, but I think we're going to pass."

"You sure? I can guarantee it'll taste like nothing you ever had before."

"Oh, I have no doubt you're right about that, my friend, but Kibble here just ate, and you know me, I'm not the biggest fan of sewer food."

"Well, I suppose that's a good thing. It leaves more for me."

Sam happily clicked her lunchbox shut when, from out of nowhere, do you know who came charging at her? Red. Red's a squirrel friend of mine. Over the years that I've gotten to know him, I suppose it's safe to say he can be a tiny bit forgetful about little things, like how many cups of coffee he drinks in a day.

Now I'm no expert, but judging from the rate of speed Red was gaining toward us, and the way his eyes looked while waving and screaming at the top of his lungs, I would say he had quite a bit of coffee that day.

"PEANUT! Oh, give me the peanut. Peanut, peanut, PEANUT! Come on, give me the peanut."

Red nearly knocked Sam to the ground, and that peanut-shaped lunchbox of hers flew into the air. Ooo-ooh-wee! I never saw a tussle like that. In the end, Sam kept her lunchbox by holding it as high as she could from Red. That is until Red realized he could climb Sam like a tree.

"Red—ow! Stop it."

Red stopped and slid back to the ground at hearing his name.

"Sorry, Sam—sometimes I get a little carried away."

"It's okay, Red, but—this is not a peanut. This is my lunchbox. It contains my lunch."

All three of us waited for her words to sink in with Red and it sure did look like they might, but then he looked at the lunchbox, blinked, and started jumping for it all over again. Well, I think that was all Sam could take that morning because she turned to us and said...

"I should go. Nice meeting you, Kibble. Good Luck."

Red, of course, followed Sam, and I must admit, Kibble and I shared a smile as we heard Red in the distance still screaming for that peanut lunchbox.

It was also around this time that I noticed something...

"Hey, Kibble, look! You shed your first skin. Congratulations."

I thought Kibble would be happy about seeing his old skin, but he seemed to me a little uneasy about the whole thing. So, to take his mind off of it, I jumped on another milkweed and bent it down for him to eat. When I did, he asked me another question.

"What did Sam mean when she said three to four weeks?"

"That's about how long it takes for you to get your wings, little buddy."

"And you're sure there's no way to avoid that, right?"

"If I didn't know better, I'd think you were a little worried about heading up."

"That would be silly, right? A caterpillar afraid of flying."

"Well, yes and no. A caterpillar afraid of flying—that isn't so silly, but if that caterpillar became a butterfly and was still afraid of flying—well then, that would worry me."

"Why? Why would that worry you?

"Well, butterflies are amazing. They enter a career right up there with bees. They're pollinators and that is something to be very proud of, my friend. Without you, none of this would be possible."

I began pointing out all the flowers and fruit hanging in the trees. Between you and me, I knew the sight would impress, but I don't think Kibble believed it. He even asked me if I was joking.

So I explained to him that when bees and butterflies fly from flower to flower for liquid food called nectar, they also pick up and leave off flower pollen. It's this pollen—which sort of looks like dust, that allows flowers to make seeds and fruit. Fruit that I love to eat, I might add.

> "So now you can see why I would worry if there was a butterfly afraid to fly because that butterfly would have a real struggle doing all of this walking from flower to flower. There's nothing wrong with a little struggle, mind you, but in this case, that struggle would seem—what's that word you used—'silly.' Yes, it would seem silly to do all that struggling, when flying would make everything easier."

Kibble was deep in thought at this point. I know when I'm thinking, I like things to be quiet. So I broke off a few milkweed leaves and handed them to him.

I was trying real hard not to talk while he sorted out whatever it was he was sorting, but then that feeling came over me again—that one I felt earlier flying way up there in the sky. Only now, I knew what that feeling was and I got so excited that I just couldn't stay quiet any longer.

> "Why, I knew this place looked familiar."

> "Excuse me?"

> "This place. I can't believe I didn't notice it earlier. Would you believe I was born around here?"

> "Really?"

"Yes siree! But I wasn't born on a milkweed leaf like you, I was born in a nest high up in—let me see here—there, that tree right there. Come on, let's walk. I remember Mama used to make Sis and me a warm meal every day and when she'd leave to do so, I would stretch my neck to see out over our nest. I would get so inspired by what I saw that I'd just start singing and singing."

"What did you see?"

"All sorts of things. Come on, I'll show you."

I hopped on the first branch of that large oak tree. Kibble seemed unsure whether to follow me or not, but then, to my surprise, he put the last of the milkweed in his mouth and carefully climbed the trunk to where I was. He held tight to that trunk at first, but after a moment or two, he slowly walked over to the branch I was sitting on. We sat there together looking at all the flowers before us.

"Now it isn't exactly what I saw when I was young, but you get the idea. It's even better from up there. Don't get me wrong, there are great colors down here too, but up there, it's different somehow. You get the bigger picture of it all. Why, I still catch myself singing when I see colors like that."

"Really?"

"Yes indeed. Whew! Long day. I think I'm going to hit the ol' branch and catch some shut eye."

"I'm not tired at all."

"That doesn't surprise me. Hey, you know something? You climbed higher than the milkweed plants—well, all except that one. Say, wouldn't that be a nice place to have a snack and watch the moon tonight? You're on your own with that one, though, because I'm way too tired. Goodnight, little buddy."

"Goodnight, Larry."

I flew up to that branch I had pointed out to Kibble earlier and
fell fast asleep. The next morning was so beautiful, that I just had
to sing. Now, I didn't know it, but Kibble was shouting to me from
that tall milkweed plant, and since there was no telling when I
would stop singing, you know what that Kibble did? He climbed the
tree all the way up to the branch I was singing from.

"Good Morning, Larry."

"Hey, Kibble, I was hoping I'd get to see you today. I hope I wasn't disturbing you. I just felt like singing. Come on over here and have a seat. I want to show you something."

It took Kibble a few moments before he was ready to let go of that trunk again, but soon enough, he carefully walked over to me. He was concentrating so hard on what he was doing that he didn't even notice all the flowers in the morning sunshine until he sat down next to me.

"Look at that—the bigger picture. Didn't I tell you it was beautiful?"

"It sure is."

"The glare from the sun gets in the eyes a bit here, though. I actually prefer that branch up there—it's my favorite branch. Come on, let's head down and get some breakfast."

I had pointed to an even higher branch than the one we were on, but to my surprise, that evening, Kibble joined me on my favorite branch.

We had a great day hanging together and Kibble shed another skin, too. Well, the sun was setting and we were just sitting there talking when Kibble said something very personal to me.

"Larry—I'm afraid I'm not going to make a very good butterfly."

"Why would you say that, little buddy?"

"I guess I'm just so—scared of it all."

"It's okay to be afraid. There's nothing wrong with that, Kid. No, nothing wrong with that at all, but do you know one of the things I like most about you?"

"What?"

"You're brave in spite of feeling scared. You, Kibble, are the bravest caterpillar I have ever met."

"I am?"

"Sure! You don't even have your wings yet, and look at you. You're sitting way up here with me. How many other caterpillars do you see crazy enough to do a thing like that?"

"Not too many, I guess."

I could tell by the smile on Kibble's face that he felt a lot better. Fear—it sure is a kicker. I reckon the hardest part about fear is getting the courage to face it. Once you do that, there isn't much fear can do—nope, not much to it, really.

"Hey Larry, I've been meaning to ask you something."

"Shoot, Kid."

"Do you think it would be all right if I made my chrysalis up here next to you?"

"Why, I'd like that. I'd like that very much."

Now, several days, and several skin sheddings later, Kibble was sitting next to me on our favorite branch watching the sunset. We had gotten to be good friends and I must admit, I liked hanging with the little guy.

One evening, though, Kibble was very quiet. I figured it was because of my yammering on and on as usual, but I just couldn't help telling him of all my adventures in the sky, or the fun I had with him over the past few days. I guess I must have worn the little guy out because his eyes looked real tired.

> "You know, I've never said this before, Kibble, but if I had to choose, I'd pick up here any day over down there. Just look at that sunset."

It wasn't like Kibble not to answer, so I turned to look at him. When I did, I saw that he was hanging upside down in the very spot where he wanted to make his chrysalis. Well, my heart started pounding, because I knew the time had come for Kibble to make his home so he could turn into a butterfly. I can tell you now, I was a little afraid myself.

> "Oh Kid, uh—now don't you worry about a thing. Everything's going to be okay. Just keep spinning that silk to hang from, and I'll be right here. I won't let anything happen to you. Just take all the time you need."

> "Hey, Larry?"

> "Yeah?"

> "Thank You."

> "You're welcome, Kid. My pleasure."

It's amazing what two little words like 'thank you' can do for someone. It made me feel great and over the next few days while Kibble was in his chrysalis, I had a wonderful time making sure he was safe and well-taken care of.

I sang to him, and made sure the rain didn't get to him. Why, I even rescued him from a very close call with Red, my squirrel friend you met earlier. Even though Kibble's chrysalis was jade green in color, Red thought it might be a peanut. When I explained to him that it was Kibble inside, boy, did we have a good laugh over that one.

I stayed on that branch with Kibble day and night and all sorts of friends wandered by visiting us. Sam even re-routed her morning walk to the yard.

"How's the Kid today, Larry?"

"He's doing just fine, just fine, indeed."

"Good to hear. Give him my best. I should get going before Red spots my lunchbox."

"You know, you could just get a different lunchbox, Sam."

"Yes, that's true—but I love this lunchbox. It's perfect for sewer surprises. I'm not sure I want to change."

"Change is the very nature of life, my friend—the very nature of life."

We waved goodbye and when I turned back, I sure was surprised, because there was Kibble. He was a little sleepy, but he had a brand new set of wings.

"Hey! Look at you."

"They're so heavy."

"You'll get used to them. They just need to dry out a bit. Keep fanning them like your doing and you'll be fine. You've done great, Kid. They look real nice."

"Thanks. I can't wait to try them out."

"Well now, isn't that music to my ears. Not scared anymore?"

"Oh I'm a little nervous, but with friends like you, I know I'm going to be all right."

The End

FUN FACTS

Some caterpillars eat only one kind of plant or a few closely related plants. This is called being "host specific". Monarch caterpillars are host specific because they only eat milkweed.

"Basking" is the term used to describe butterflies warming themselves in the sun.

Butterflies can smell through their feet.

Does that mean I have smelly feet?

The largest butterfly is the female Queen Alexandra's Birdwing. Its wingspan can measure roughly 1 foot. One of the smallest butterflies is the Pygmy Blue (pronounced PIG-me). Its wingspan can measure roughly a 1/2 inch.

gulp

You can say that again!

You're stepping on my thorax.

It's cold today.

Excuse me.

Oops.

A Monarch "Roost" is a group of Monarch butterflies huddled together for rest or to stay warm.

The Monarch butterfly makes a two-way migration like birds do. Some travel as far as 3,000 miles to reach their winter home and a full migration cycle can take 3-4 generations to complete.

THE LIFE CYCLE OF BUTTERFLIES AND MOTHS

Stage 1: Egg

Stage 2: Larva

Stage 3: Pupa At this stage, our body structure changes into something different. This process is called Metamorphosis.

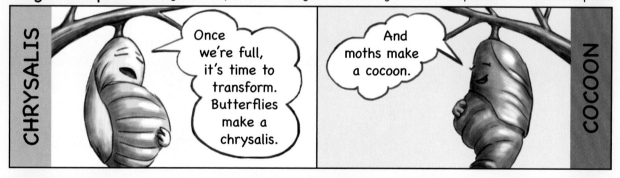

Stage 4: Adult

*Not all caterpillars feed on leaves. For example, the Lycaenid caterpillar feeds upon ant larvae.

HOW A MONARCH CATERPILLAR
FORMS A CHRYSALIS

Beginning
The caterpillar chooses a location and spins a silk button to hang from while it sheds its final skin.

Middle
A black post called a cremaster hooks around the skin and attaches to the silk button. This is a very critcal stage because if the skin doesn't fall, the butterfly will be deformed.

End
The chrysalis hardens into a jade green color for Monarch butterflies. Metamorphosis continues until the butterfly is ready to emerge.

THE PROCESS OF
POLLINATION

Monarch caterpillars only eat Milkweed leaves, but Monarch butterflies enjoy nectar (liquid food) from many types of flowers.

While they drink flower nectar, tiny ball-like grains known as flower pollen stick to their legs.

When they leave a flower to drink nectar from another like flower, the pollen on their legs rubs off onto the new flower. This process is known as cross-pollination and it allows flowers to form seeds and fruit.

DUE

	PRINTED IN U.S.A.